ROSIE'S WALK

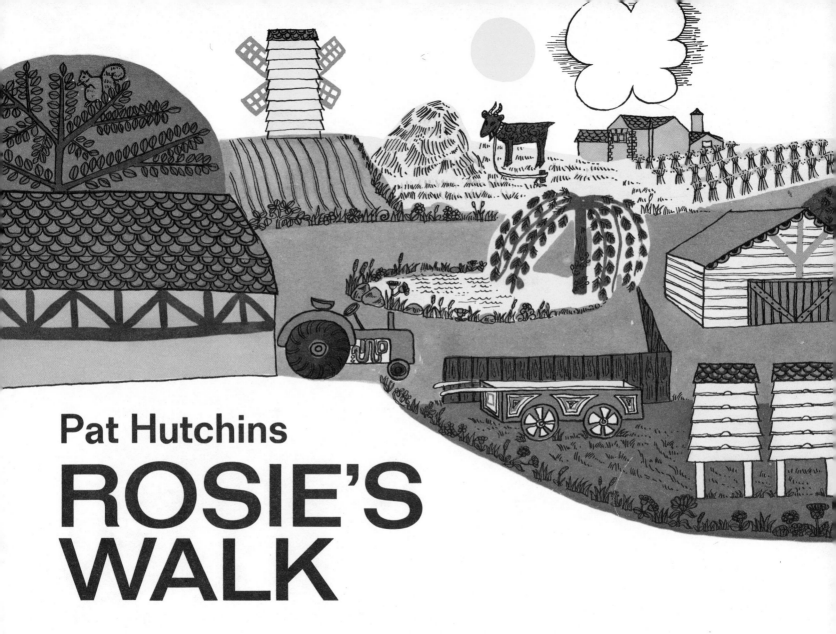

Pat Hutchins

ROSIE'S WALK

SCHOLASTIC INC.

New York Toronto London Auckland Sydney

ISBN 0-590-41239-6

27 26 25 24 23 22 21   8 9/9

Printed in the U.S.A.   08
First Scholastic printing, September 1987

For
Wendy
and
Stephen

Rosie the hen went for a walk

across the yard

around
the
pond

over the haystack

past the mill

through the fence

under the beehives

and
got back
in time
for dinner.